A JOURNEY TO POWER

A CLEAN YA EPIC FANTASY ADVENTURE

DEFENDERS OF THE REALM
BOOK 0.5

MARIE-HÉLÈNE LEBEAULT

BEACHES AND TRAILS
PUBLISHING

ABOUT THE AUTHOR

Marie-Helene Lebeault lives in Quebec, Canada and is the mother of two young adults. A retired teacher, she now spends her days writing, translating academic manuals, and lending her voice to corporate training videos. She enjoys reading, hiking, and going to the beach. She is also an avid rollercoaster fiend and is on a mission to visit all the Six Flags amusement parks with her daughter. Every year, she travels for three weeks on a solo adventure to a new part of the world.

Follow on Social Media, She'd love to hear from you!

Website Email Newsletter

facebook.com/mhlebeaultauthor

x.com/mhlebeault

instagram.com/mhlebeault

amazon.com/author/mhlebeault

bookbub.com/authors/marie-helene-lebeault

goodreads.com/mhlebeault

linkedin.com/in/mhlebeault

tiktok.com/@mhlebeaultauthor

youtube.com/@mhlebeault

ALSO BY THE AUTHOR

Blood Magick Trilogy

The Blood Mage

Blood Magick

Blood Legacy

Standalones

Clarity Castle

What Happens Next?

Ghost Stories

Holiday Shifters

Echoes of Tomorrow

Utopia

Picture Books

Fairy Grandmother: Millie Goes to Antarctica

Fairy Grandmother: Millie Goes to the North Pole

Fairy Grandmother: Millie Goes to China

Fairy Grandmother: Millie Goes to Africa

(Also available in French, Spanish, German, and Italian)

CHAPTER

ONE

Wickham frowned as he checked his bag for the fourth time. Mother and Father repeatedly told him that the Crown would provide everything needed for the trip to Silver Springs, but one couldn't be too careful.

However, half of what he had packed now mysteriously disappeared.

The thirteen-year-old lifted his bag, thinking maybe some of it had fallen out. When he heard whimpering from under his bed, though, he knew what had happened. With a sigh, he sat on the edge of his bed, taking in the cluttered room he shared with his ten-year-old twin brothers.

"I really hope my belongings come back," he said aloud. "If they don't, then I'll have to go without them."

The small voice of Wickham's youngest sibling, two-year-old Tara, answered, "Wick, stay."

"Did I hear something?" Wickham wrinkled his nose as though confused before he knelt beside his bed. A peek below revealed Tara and the missing items. Tara's big brown eyes stared at him. But

Wickham pretended not to see her; it was her favorite game, after all. "Oh, look at that! How did everything get here?"

Tara tried to pout but giggled as Wickham pulled his things out and pretended he didn't see her. Soon enough, she crawled out and climbed onto his bed.

"Wick stay," she insisted.

Wickham tied his long brown hair into a ponytail. "You know I must go, Tara. I've graduated from basics, and now that I'm thirteen, I need to see if I'm a witch, a dragon, or a human."

Even though he maintained a smile for his sister's sake, his heart tugged. Yes, he had the basics of reading, writing, math, and other necessities all children in Eldavon received. But he didn't feel ready to leave his family for this quest.

He had the skills to complete the journey. But his family had just moved into town. His mother had started a new job with the seamstress, and his father was working long hours to buy a larger house...

Wickham's shoulders hunched forward. Maybe he could put it off one more year. There were forms they could fill out for that, weren't there? Accommodations made for children who were sick or otherwise unable to make the journey?

Mother came in after a knock. Tara jumped off the bed and ran to her, burying her face in Mother's apron.

"Mama, Wick stay home," she pleaded.

"Now, Tara," Mother said, crouching to her daughter. "This is an important journey for Wick. It's his right to go to Silver Springs. You'll be able to go when you're thirteen, too."

"Me two!" Tara protested. She held up two fingers with her face scrunched up, looking terribly offended.

Mother laughed and kissed Tara's forehead. "Supper is ready. Go on and wash your hands."

Tara seemed to forget about Wickham's impending departure as she clapped her chubby hands and skipped off.

Wickham fidgeted. "Maybe I should wait another year."

"Wick, come here." Mother held her arms out to him. Wickham stepped into her embrace. "You think you must be here to look after your younger siblings because you worry about them. But we have everything well in hand."

"But with you and Father working so much—"

Mother shook her head. "No, no. Don't start thinking about that, dearest. We have the village, and we have support from the Crown. We will take care of everything."

"Traveling to the castle and back takes an entire month. Then the journey—" Wickham was cut off as Mother tapped his nose.

"The journey will only take another month. Everything will be fine, Wickham. You might be the oldest of your siblings, but their care is not your responsibility."

Wickham heaved a sigh. Mother and Father always said that. But he couldn't help worrying... would they really be all right without him?

SWEAT DRIPPED down Penelope's back as she completed the last pushup of her morning routine. Her muscles burned with the pleasant, post-exercise exertion. Her long red hair was braided into a bun at the back of her head.

On either side of her, her mother and father also finished their exercises. Momma's short silver hair stuck up at all angles. It had been as red as Penelope's before she drank from the stream and was revealed to be a witch.

Her dad's hair was a lot like Penelope's. His glowing silver eyes, which marked him as a dragon, pinched at the corners in a smile.

"Can't we start the journey a day early?" she asked her parents as they headed for the lake they were camped next to.

Her parents were part of the Fire Watch this year. They had been traveling through the forests, clearing out underbrush with the other watch members, and dealing with any forest fires that needed to be put out. It was a delicate balance between letting nature run its course and protecting the land where people lived.

Da chuckled as he waded into the lake. "Pen, we've talked about this. Your mother and I must finish our shifts here before we can leave."

"It will only take a week to get to the castle," Momma reminded her. "And we must wait for Julie and Benton to get here."

Penelope dove into the clear waters, letting the lake muffle the sounds of life around her. Her older siblings would come with them for the journey. They would wait at the barracks where others of the Fire Watch would be while the children climbed to the mountain's peak.

Her brother and sister were both revealed to be dragons when they drank from the stream. Penelope already knew she would be as well. Her parents did, too, even though they kept reminding Penelope that the magic didn't work that way. The magic decided if you were human, witch, or dragon. Not you.

It didn't matter if her father and siblings were dragons or if her mother was a witch. There was very little evidence to suggest it mattered who your family was. King Lantos, for instance, though he was dragon, had only humans in his family. Most children born to witches and dragons were human. It was odd that both her older siblings were dragons. It would be even odder if she were as well.

All of them expected it, though. Even if it would be an oddity, the family often slipped into referring to 'when' Penelope would be a dragon, not 'if.' Perhaps because she wanted it so badly.

Penelope's gut clenched as she cut through the cold water, pushing her burning muscles harder.

What if she wasn't a dragon? What purpose would she serve if she didn't follow in her father's and siblings' footsteps? They were a family who all worked in the Fire Watch. If she were a witch, she could still work with the family...

But humans weren't part of the Watch. If she was a human, what would become of her? Yes, humans trained for trades necessary for the Kingdom's survival. There were farmers, carpenters, diplomats, teachers, and record keepers. It wasn't as though humans were less than dragons or witches; all jobs were vital.

Penelope broke through the surface of the water and breathed in the sweet mountain air.

All the same, if she weren't a dragon... she'd be disappointed. She knew her parents would be, too, even though they would never say it.

This journey can't be over fast enough, she thought as she started a backstroke. *I want to get back to normal.*

CHAPTER
TWO

The stairs seemed to go on forever. Kaia stared up in determination and despair. She was determined not to fall behind the other children when they started their journey up the mountain to the Silver Springs. But so far, it appeared her training had come too little, too late.

She sat on the first step with a sigh, her skirt floating about her.

"It's all right, take your time," her language tutor, Madame Adora, said.

Like Kaia, Madame Adora had short legs and a squat waist. She had been the one to suggest that Kaia march up and down the stairs of the family palace every day to prepare for the journey. Kaia had diligently been training every day since the end of winter.

Up the stairs, down the stairs. Up, reciting poetry; down, practicing her languages. Up, memorizing timetables; down, reminding herself of significant historical events. Climb to the second floor. Rest. Climb to the third floor. Rest. Climb to the fourth floor. Admire the view. Then down again. She'd counted the stairs so many times that she had them memorized. Twenty-five steps between the floors. Seventy-five in total. They built the palace to hold lots of visitors, after all.

Up and down, up and down, until she made herself grow dizzy over time.

Kaia's legs seemed stronger now than when she first started. These days, she could go from dungeon to attic and back four times before her muscles shook.

It didn't feel like enough.

She accepted the sandwich Madame Adora handed her and gratefully scarfed it down. "When will Mama and Papa be home again?"

"They said they would be back for suppertime, my little button," Madame Adora replied.

Summer was always hectic for her parents; they were a dragon-witch duo who had been assigned to the agricultural district. They had to check the various farmlands across the Kingdom for disease, drought, and other potential problems.

Kaia hated travel. She was much happier staying in the palace, reading or strolling and shopping through town.

"Perhaps we should go to the stores tomorrow and get you some traveling clothes," Madame Adora mused. "You will need some sturdy trousers to traverse the mountain paths."

"Ugh. I hate trousers," Kaia complained. She flicked her short curls out of her eyes.

She'd always hated the dull yellow color of her hair and had already determined to dye it as soon as the summer was over. She was thirteen and a graduate from school, after all. Many children her age were already entering trades or taking on summer jobs; why couldn't she change her hair color?

Her parents were always telling her to love the body she was given. Kaia didn't see why she couldn't love her body while also wanting to change certain things.

"Trousers are more practical than skirts," Madame Adora told her gently.

"Maybe, but I still hate them. I hate the way they cling to my legs. They feel so suffocating," Kaia complained.

She stood and rolled her shoulders. As she looked up the stairs, she imagined a muddy mountain path. Then, she looked down at her beautiful rose-pink skirt and frowned.

"I need trousers," she decided. "I don't want to get any of my pretty clothes ruined in the forest. Besides, I can do anything I set my mind to. I can wear trousers just fine."

She started up the stairs again, determined she would not let herself down. Kaia was an only child. Since all of her cousins were touched by magic... and if she were, too, she might end up taking on hard jobs. She had to prepare herself for that. She had to be ready to do things she didn't want to do.

Wearing trousers, as awful as they were, was an excellent step in preparing herself for her future.

THE LIBRARIAN LOOKED over the stack of books Herja was checking out and clicked her tongue. "Do you really read these?"

"Yes," Herja replied.

Life at the orphanage afforded Herja plenty of time to read. Chores, schoolwork, and social events were the only things that got in her way. Luckily, there weren't many children who couldn't be placed in homes. Herja was one of the unlucky ones, or so the state believed.

For herself, she preferred having the structure of the orphanage. Her caretakers weren't her parents, so she didn't feel obligated to make them proud. Not having the complication of family had undoubtedly given her a head start on planning her future.

"I don't think I've ever seen a young person read more than you," the librarian said, chuckling. "You're turning thirteen this year, right?"

"I already turned thirteen, just yesterday," Herja replied.

The librarian smiled. Herja knew her name but preferred to think of her in vague terms; it prevented emotional connections.

"Happy birthday! I would have gotten a present for you if I'd known."

Herja rested her elbows on the checkout counter, watching as the librarian scanned each book. "Why? I'm nobody to you."

The librarian frowned. "No child is nobody, Herja. Especially not one who has frequented the library every single day for at least four years."

"It's only because there are books here."

The librarian shook her head. "You are a prickly customer, aren't you?"

Herja shrugged. "That's the way I like it. People just get in my way."

"Do they?"

"They do."

Whether this summer saw her become a dragon, witch, or human, Herja knew precisely what she would do. She had planned it all out. After five years at the orphanage, she would leave. Technically, she should stay until she was either enrolled in a school that would enable her or support herself, but Herja wasn't spending another year here.

She was thirteen years old, about to take the sacred journey to discover her fate, and she was ready to move on.

She hadn't graduated from basics two years early for nothing. It wasn't until this year that she could get a job outside the orphanage, but she had been studying and teaching herself everything she needed to succeed.

"What happens when you are matched with your fated mate, then?" the librarian asked. She put the books in Herja's pack. "*They're* going to be a person."

Herja wrinkled her nose. "I won't have one."

"Oh? You're certain you're human, then?"

"It doesn't matter if I'm a dragon or a witch. I don't want a fated mate. They'd just get in my way." Herja tested her pack and nodded. It was a little heavy, but nothing she couldn't handle. "I'll be late in returning these books. I'm taking them on the sacred journey."

The librarian's eyes widened. As Herja turned, she called out, "Wait!"

Herja pursed her lips and turned again. "What?"

"Give me back those books. I've got something that will work better for you," the librarian said.

Herja hesitated before she set the pack on the counter again. With one hand, the librarian tucked her silvery hair behind her ears as she pulled a drawstring bag from behind the counter. She laid it down and lifted a cup of sweet-smelling water over it.

"This is a spell I learned while I was at the Institute," she said, sprinkling water over it. She chanted something in a low voice, and the droplets of water glowed.

Herja watched in fascination as stitched vines crept over her bag. Once a flower seemed to blossom in the middle, the librarian sprinkled some powder that soaked up the water instantly.

"There. Hang it up to dry in the sunshine, and then this haversack will hold all these books at a fraction of the weight. You'll want to travel light up that mountain," the librarian held out the bag. She smiled at Herja. "Happy birthday."

Moisture pooled in Herja's eyes, and a lump rose in her throat. She grabbed the bag and her books and left the library before her tears could fall.

She would not miss this place.

She wouldn't let herself.

CHAPTER
THREE

The palace was in the center of the Kingdom, built at the base of Mount Eldavon, the Kingdom's namesake. It was a sprawling building with four wings, one for each major branch of the government. The central area housed the living quarters of the two couples that ruled the lands.

All the thirteen-year-old children from the Kingdom and their guardians were milling about in the courtyard at the start of the path that wound up Mount Eldavon to the sacred Silver Springs.

Herja scoffed when she saw the sign that read 'Your Journey Begins Here' next to the path. With a sign like that, you'd expect it to be lined with manicured hedges and composed of intricately cut stones. It was a regular dirt path, about four feet wide, the kind you see when beginning most hikes.

How long do we have to wait? Herja thought, attempting to keep herself from fidgeting like so many children she saw around her.

"There have been human-human pairs and a witch-dragon pairs since the Covenant was first struck," Herja told Mr. Bryce, one of the orphanage caretakers. They insisted that a caretaker go with her, even though she had planned the trip alone. She was annoyed at having to adjust her plan to allow Mr. Bryce to accompany her.

She was the only orphan who turned thirteen this year, and they didn't think she could do it on her own for some weird reason.

"What's the Covenant again?" he asked.

Herja tapped her toes against the large flagstones that paved the castle's courtyard. Everyone knew what the Covenant was. But talking about it helped to make her feel less antsy for her journey to begin.

Why do we have to stand around talking, anyway? Herja huffed and folded her arms. "It was the pact made long ago that every person in the Kingdom would have the chance to drink from the stream. We named witches, dragons, and humans at every level of government so that all would have their interests protected."

"And?" Mr. Bryce pressed.

Herja sighed. "And what? That's why we have prospered for over a thousand years. There are checks and balances to any one person's power, preventing abuse of said power. It's why we have enough food and resources to care for everyone.

Mr. Bryce smiled at her. "Herja, Herja, Herja. You have more skills than just that steel trap of a mind you have, you know."

"What does that mean?" Herja complained.

"It means that—Oh!" Mr. Bryce put a hand on her shoulder. "Look! It's them."

THE FOUR RULERS of Eldavon stood before the thirty-six children taking part in this year's journey. The children's guardians waited with them as the kings and queens beamed at them. Penelope stood near the edge of the group, surrounded by her parents and siblings. As the youngest, she had stood through their opening remarks before, but this was the first time she wanted to pay attention.

"Welcome, young people of Eldavon," the dragon king, King Lantos, said. He stepped forward. His silver eyes glowed as he looked over the crowd. His silver crown and bald head both glinted in the morning light. "We are pleased to see you here."

Penelope straightened herself as the king's eyes swept over to where she and her family stood. She knew it was ridiculous to think that he would recognize them since the rulers saw dozens of families yearly. But she couldn't help but feel like his smile widened for her.

"We know you must be excited to get going," King Lantos continued. "We will keep this as brief as possible, but you must know a few things about how this proceeds."

Penelope ground her teeth as her impatience flared. "Everyone knows how this goes," she muttered.

Momma tapped her shoulder, silently showing that she needed to calm herself.

"Psst," Julie whispered, bending slightly to Penelope's level. "Just because you have older siblings that went through this doesn't mean everyone else does. Look at that boy over there. He's hanging on every word."

Penelope glanced at the brown-haired boy standing next to a grandmotherly-looking woman. He held himself utterly rigid, staring straight ahead as though he would have to recite King Lantos' words.

"But he had to have parents and grandparents that would tell him," Penelope hissed back to her sister.

Momma tapped her shoulder again.

"Today is a day of celebration," King Lantos said, spreading his arms wide. He wore a simple black shirt, trousers, and a sword.

Penelope had never seen a sword up close. She imagined for a moment being a dragon in military service rather than a firefighter. A thrill and chill shot through her, and she pushed the thought away. She would be on the Fire Watch like the rest of her family.

All the rulers dressed simply. Queen Johanna wore green, King Diesel wore blue, and Queen Charlize wore beige. Other than the color, all their clothes were precisely the same, similar to what people in the Fire Watch wore. King Lantos was the only one who had a sword, though.

King Lantos turned his palms upward toward the sun. "Tomorrow, you will take the first steps of your journey, leaving behind your families to make your way to the Silver Springs and—"

A high, clear voice suddenly called out, interrupting the King. "Why can't we leave right now?"

Penelope craned her neck, jaw-dropping. Murmurs burst out around her, along with some nervous titters. Who would be so rude as to interrupt the King like that?

WICKHAM PRESSED CLOSER TO MOTHER, hoping to put distance between himself and the black-haired girl who had just yelled out.

At the King.

The King!

"What are you doing?" he hissed. "You don't yell at the King!"

The girl turned pale, baleful eyes on him. "It's a waste of time to stand around for another full day when we can start the journey right now."

Wickham stared at her, wondering what was wrong with her. The crowd parted, and one of the dragon guards stepped forward, looking between them.

"Which of you two asked?" the guard asked.

The girl stuck her chin out. "I did. And I'm waiting for an answer."

Wickham shrank behind Mother, hoping that the guard would believe the girl. Yes, it was the truth, but that didn't stop him from feeling guilty.

"Herja," admonished the girl's... father? Maybe, though, they looked nothing like each other.

The girl, Herja, folded her arms and remained staring at the guard. "Well?"

Her father looked at the sky and closed his eyes, as adults do when their patience was tested. What was wrong with that girl? Didn't she know they needed to have all the help they could to ensure this journey was a success?

"Herja, was it?" the guard said, kneeling to her level.

"Yes," Herja replied.

"King Lantos would like to speak with you. Will you come with me, please? You and your father?"

"Caretaker," the girl said, throwing her shoulders back. "I don't have a father."

The man with them murmured something to the guard, who nodded. Silently, the guard led the two back through the crowd to where the rulers were. The two humans, King Diesel and Queen Charlize had both been given chairs, which was understandable considering their white hair and wrinkled faces.

Queen Johanna, King Lantos' mate, and their witch-ruler

looped her arm through his as Herja and her caretaker stopped before them.

"What's your name?" the queen asked kindly.

"Herja. And I'm going to ask again, why do we have to waste time on all this talk when we could start the journey tonight?" Herja asked.

Now that he knew he would not get in trouble, Wickham had to admit that he was likewise curious. The faster the journey took place, the faster he could get home. Father must be having a hard time dealing with the twins and Tara on his own, especially since he had to take time off work while Mother came with him to the castle...

"I can understand your excitement, Herja," King Lantos said, smiling at her.

Wickham relaxed. He should have known better than to think Herja would get in trouble. The kings and queens had been chosen to fulfill their roles because of their even tempers and kind hearts.

Herja, in front of everyone, tossed her short black hair. "It's not excitement. It's impatience."

"We all have things to learn, Herja, from the ceremonies," Queen Johanna said.

"But I already know everything. We will take the path to the mountain's peak. I know it will take three days, and the stop points for each night will have cabins, where we will restock our food and water and have a good night's sleep for the next day. They will teach us the history and all that."

King Lantos knelt, chuckling. "You know, you remind me of myself when I was thirteen. Despite thinking I knew it all, I learned something significant from the ceremonies."

Wickham squinted. What would he have to learn?

"Patience," King Lantos continued.

People around them laughed, but as Herja opened her mouth,

closed it, then ducked her head and hurried back into the crowd, Wickham frowned. He tugged on his mother's sleeve. "She seems upset."

"I think she feels like she made a mistake," Mother replied.

"Maybe she needs a friend," Wickham decided.

The three-day journey they would take would give him time to figure out if she did, he thought. He smiled. Maybe other people needed his help besides his family.

FOUR

K aia hardly slept that night. All the children slept under the large canopy set up in the courtyard. She wasn't used to sharing such close quarters with strangers.

She tried to think of her parents' stories of their journey to Silver Springs and how wonderful it felt to know one's true purpose in life.

"No matter what the Silver Springs sees in you, you will know where you belong," Mama told her, braiding her hair the next morning. "Whether a protective dragon, a healing witch, or a clever human."

Kaia giggled. "What if I become a clever dragon or a healing human?"

"Then we will be even more proud of you," Papa said. He tickled under Kaia's chin, making her giggle.

Kaia picked up her pack filled with food and water for the day and pulled it onto her shoulders. It was heavier than she expected. But she had been practicing walking the stairs, so this was going to be easy... right?

She swallowed, trying hard to hide her nerves. Her stomach was a swarm of butterflies, but she didn't want to seem silly about being apprehensive over such a fantastic day. Her mind raced with all the possibilities of her future.

All around them, other parents were helping their children prepare—so many heads of silver hair or glowing silver eyes. Of course, the number of humans outnumbered both witches and dragons. The chances were Kaia would be human, too, although all of her extended family was magical.

"If I am human," she said slowly, "I will study my languages extra hard and maybe work as a translator for the sailing merchants."

Mama beamed. "That sounds lovely, dearest."

The two kings and queens walked through the crowds, murmuring a few words to each child before moving on. Queen Charlize approached Kaia, leaning heavily on her cane.

Kaia welcomed the queen with a hug. Her parents worked closely with the Crown in the agricultural sector, which Queen Charlize was head of; Kaia had spent many years having tea parties with the queen as her parents gave their reports.

"Oh, my," the queen said, hugging her back. "What are you doing here, Kaia? It's not time for you yet. You're only five."

Kaia laughed. Charlize liked to tease her like that. "Oh, but don't you remember? You said I could go to Silver Springs early. I have the letter right here."

She pantomimed, pulling a letter from her pocket and showing it to Charlize, who pretended to take the paper and look it over.

"I don't think this is my signature at all," she said.

"You're getting old," Kaia said sadly, shaking her head. "Can't even remember it."

Charlize laughed and hugged her again. "Good luck, Kaia. If I can give you a blessing?"

"I would love it," Kaia replied.

Charlize put her hands on either of Kaia's shoulders, smiling down at her. "May you find the path that will lead to your fulfillment, a path that will show you where your strengths best lie, and friends that will be with you forever."

The queen kissed Kaia's forehead. Kaia beamed at her as she moved to the next group.

"A path that will show me where my strengths best lie," Kaia repeated. "I wonder what that means...."

She didn't have long to ponder because, soon enough, everyone was heading toward the mountain. Kaia held Mama and Papa's hands tightly as they headed off.

Then, with one last hug and kiss from each of her parents, they were off! Kaia was nervous that she would be left behind, unable to keep up with everyone else. A muscular girl, Penelope, walked at the front of the group and set their pace. She kept them going at a pace Kaia could easily keep up with.

At midday, they stopped next to a tumbling little stream with clear water that showed smooth rocks beneath. Kaia quickly stripped her shoes and socks off to stick them into the cool water.

The stiff boy she had seen at the welcoming ceremony sat beside her. Kaia splashed her toes in the water as they opened their packs to eat.

"I'm Kaia," she greeted.

He looked at her, then looked away. "Nolen."

"I'm pleased to meet you. Isn't this a beautiful spot?" Kaia asked. She tilted her face toward the sun. "It reminds me of a story I read about a girl who was lost in the wilderness for a year before she was found. This is just the sort of giggling brook she would set camp next to, and every morning she would wash her face and drink her fill in its cool, crystal waters."

Nolen stared at her. "You can't do that. Boil the water, or you could get sick."

"Do you?" Kaia asked, her eyes widening. "But we never boil water at home."

"Where do you get your water from?"

"The well."

Nolen huffed. "But do you drink directly from the well?"

Kaia thought a moment. "No," she finally said. "I get it from the decanter my tutors fill for me."

"There you have it. Other people boil it first." Nolen bit into his sandwich.

"Oh. I didn't know that." Kaia grinned at her new friend. "Thank you for telling me."

Nolen looked a little startled. "Er... welcome?"

Kaia laughed. This was already a glorious adventure!

PENELOPE WAS grateful to see the first rest stop come into view just as twilight faded into the night pitch. They hadn't made the time that she would have liked on this first leg of the journey, but at least they had lost no one—she had been counting heads at each rest point, mindful that with such a big group, it was easy to lose people—all thirty-six of them were at the cabin now.

Four adults waited for them, smiling brightly. They were all dragons, their eyes luminescent in the night. Lanterns hung at the cabin's entrance. It was more of a long hall made of logs than a cabin, but it was a place to sleep.

"Welcome, young travelers," one adult said. "My name is Miss Greta, and these are my colleagues, Mr. Cyrus, Mr. Finnigan, and

Mr. Todd. We've prepared a supper for you, and we'll be telling you how the first dragons were born while you eat."

The girl who had made such a scene at the welcoming, Herja, snorted, "Everyone knows that story. Why don't you tell us something useful?"

Irritation spiked through Penelope, and she turned to Herja. "Why don't you keep your opinions to yourself? You don't get to ruin it for everyone else just because you're bored."

She would have said more, but she bit her tongue. Her parents had always told her that maintaining one's temper was the hallmark of a dragon. Even if Penelope had difficulty keeping her cool sometimes, that didn't mean she shouldn't try.

Herja narrowed her eyes, then shrugged.

Mr. Cyrus cleared his throat. "Everyone, come along inside. We have your seats arranged already."

Penelope followed the four adults inside. Tables were set in rows with dozens of plates already on them. Each setting was marked with a child's name. She quickly found hers and sat. While the children found their spots, the adults moved down the tables, serving them steaming food.

Once everyone was eating, Miss Greta stood at the front of the room, perched on a crate. "Long ago, when the world was wild and unformed, the First Ones wandered through tumultuous terrain, fighting daily for their survival."

Penelope leaned forward, trying to hear more of the story. She knew it, of course. Herja was correct. But she loved hearing about the first dragon.

"During this time, a long winter set on the land," Miss Greta continued. "The First Ones huddled together to keep warm, but the chill stole into their bones. Their voices of pain and grief rose to the heavens, where the sun took pity on them."

She'd finished her food faster than she intended, so Penelope closed her eyes and imagined the scene being described. The First Ones huddled in a tiny group while the sun grew brighter above them. The first warmth they must have felt in so long.

"When the sun touched them, it warmed them from the inside out, and they no longer shivered. They soon found that they had been granted a second form, that of a magnificent dragon. Can anyone tell me what happened next?"

Penelope's hand shot straight into the air. "The dragons split up to find other First Ones and offer them the warmth they were blessed with. They spread over the face of the land, and with their internal fires, they drove back the winter and allowed the first spring to arrive."

Miss Greta smiled at her. "Exactly. And from that day forward, dragons knew that their gift allowed them to protect others, and they kept that sacred duty close to their hearts even until this day."

Penelope smiled. It was a sacred duty that she was sure was hers.

CHAPTER

FIVE

Herja swatted at the swarms of bugs around her, wrinkling her nose in disgust. She had thought she knew everything there was to know about this quest, but she hadn't counted on so many of these annoying, buzzing insects! They bit through the fabric of her clothes, and large, itchy bumps appeared all over her arms and legs.

It was a cool, overcast day. Herja thought that was good since they could make better time until the next rest stop without the sun beating down on them.

Unfortunately, the cooler weather, paired with slight dampness in the air, brought the bugs out in full force. Everyone was miserable as they marched steadily on.

Maybe if they walked faster? Herja was at the front of the group, but she'd kept even pace with Penelope. She thought a moment, then went quickly, hoping Penelope would unconsciously match her pace.

"Let's take a break," Penelope called.

Herja stopped and stared at her. "Really?"

"There are fewer mosquitoes here," Penelope replied as she slid her pack off. "And we've walked past midday. We need a break to eat and regain our strength."

Herja's stomach rumbled. She hadn't even noticed how hungry she had gotten, too focused on the bugs. She adjusted the weight of her pack. The thing about these stops was that they weren't long enough for her to read but were too long for her to eat and get going again.

"Why can't we just eat while we keep walking?" she asked Penelope.

Penelope took her by the elbow and pulled her to one side while the others removed their packs and found a place to sit. "See those four at the back?"

Herja craned her neck, seeing the four children at the very back. One of them, a thin boy, leaned heavily on a walking stick.

"That boy with the stick is named Robert," Penelope said. "He was sick with pneumonia for three months over the winter. He can't go any faster and needs to rest his lungs. I'm not leaving anyone behind."

"I... don't understand why the rest of us have to wait for him just because *you* want to," Herja replied stoutly.

Penelope frowned at her. "I don't understand. I heard you talking with Kaia earlier. You said you already have some magic and are sure you'll be a dragon or a witch."

Herja shrugged. "Yes. So?"

"So how do you plan on serving the people as a witch or dragon if you don't start now?"

Oh. She hadn't thought about that before. Herja's eyebrows furrowed as she took off her pack. Serving others was their sacred duty... but she didn't see how waiting for stragglers equated with serving the community.

As Herja puzzled over the question, a boy named Nolen

approached her and Penelope, carrying handfuls of some plant, which he held out to them.

"This is lemongrass," he said. "If you rub it on your skin and clothes, it will help to mask you from the mosquitos."

Herja frowned. "I've never heard of that. How do you know?"

Nolen stared at her with a severe expression. "My family is part of the guard watch near the Silent Marshes. I know mosquitoes."

He pushed the plants into her hands and walked away. Herja sniffed the lemony-scented grass. She rubbed it over her arms and neck. *We'll see if it works.*

THE SECOND NIGHT was much the same as the first; four adults welcomed them, all with silvery hair that seemed to glow in the pale night. Witches this time. The children were admitted and brought inside the long hall for a prepared meal.

Wickham shoveled food into his mouth as soon as it was set before him. He was used to working hard at home, but a few others had neglected to pack enough food the previous day; they hoped they would be fine traveling light. Wickham had shared his food with them and now was starving.

Mr. Julian stood on the stage and lifted his hands, pointing his palms toward the ceiling. "Long ago, on a night when the seas were rough, and the winds cut through the night, the First Ones slept uneasily. Their dragon protector stood guard, but he was tired. He had fought wild beasts and shielded the First Ones from the weather for weeks on end."

Wickham stretched his sore muscles, fidgeting as he continued to eat. He wasn't too familiar with this story, but it didn't matter to him.

What were Mother and Father doing? How were the twins and little Tara? Mother would still be at the palace, waiting for them to return. Tomorrow they would get to the spring and stay there for another two or three days; then, they would have the three-day journey back down the mountain again.

So, it would be another five or six days before he returned to Mother and took the long trip home.

He bit back a sigh.

"The First Ones could see that the dragon was sad, being alone. They knew it wasn't right. One from the group decided she would stay awake all night with him. Though she could not guard against the biting winds, she wrapped herself in a blanket and sat with the dragon, singing songs to keep his spirits awake."

Beside him, Herja pulled a book out of her bag. Wickham's eyebrows disappeared under his fringe of brown hair. "That's a different book than you had last night," he whispered.

Herja glanced at him. "I brought six."

"How can you carry six books!" Wickham cried a little louder than he intended.

Mr. Julian paused. Wickham ducked his head, and the witch continued, "The moon heard her voice and looked on the scene in pity."

Herja bent toward him. "You see this bag?" She pulled a beautifully embroidered drawstring bag from her pack. "It's magic. It's been enchanted to hold my books while weighing only as much as one."

"That's so cool," Wickham whispered.

An elbow poked into his side. Adina, one child who had neglected to pack correctly the previous night, glared at him. "Be quiet! I'm trying to listen."

Wickham straightened in his chair, blushing. He clasped his hands tightly together as he looked back at Mr. Julian.

"And so, the moon scoured the land for all the dragons. To encourage them to resume a human form, the Moon created witches to be their mates. Witches would act as the balancing element between dragons and humans. They held the power to heal injuries and lift the burdens of others. Sun and Moon, Dragon and Witch. A perfect match."

Wickham gazed at the silvery hair of the witches and twisted a strand of his long hair around his finger. He looked like his father. If he had sunlight or moonlight in his blood... would he still look like his father after the change?

THE THIRD DAY'S hike was the hottest and most challenging yet. Kaia's whole body ached when they reached the rest stop, even though they made it well before nightfall this time.

Unlike the previous log cabins, this one was built of stone and looked similar in design to the castle at the mountain's base. Four humans greeted them and told the children where to leave their belongings, then led them to a dining hall where food was already set out on the tables.

One human, Mr. Luca, stood before the group. "Now. I'm sure you all know what comes next."

"A long time ago," one child called out. "Before humans walked the world."

Everyone laughed.

Mr. Luca held up his hands, silencing them. He smiled, though. "Yes, exactly. Long ago, when dragons and witches roamed with the

First Ones before the first human breathed, there came a great war. No one knows exactly how it started. Some think that a witch fell in love with a dragon that was not his perfect mate who scorned his mate in favor of her. Others say it was the dragon who spurned her perfect mate."

Kaia drank from her cup eagerly, only half-listening to Mr. Luca's tale.

"Mates were torn apart, the light of both sun and moon withdrew, ashamed of the misuse they saw of their magic. The First Ones cried out in terror to see their healers fight their protectors, their protectors against their healers."

Kaia shivered, lowering her cup. It had never occurred to her before now how terrifying that would be. It would be as though Mama and Papa had come to blows with one another. *Those poor people.*

"Blood soaked the earth," Mr. Luca continued, his voice grave and sad. "The First Ones begged for the fighting to stop... but the eyes and ears of witches and dragons were shut, and their cries went unanswered."

"Until the Earth," whispered the girl sitting next to her. She leaned in close to Kaia. "The Earth heard their cries, and it cried with them."

Mr. Luca said precisely what the girl had just said, and she giggled. "He's my father, and I've been listening to him practice."

Kaia smiled at her, then focused on Mr. Luca again.

"The Earth had no light to give, but it mustered its strength and filled the blood of the First Ones with the clear flowing water and thick burning flames it held within itself. They became Humans, strong and mighty with a gift of their own." Mr. Luca paused, then took a deep breath. "With these new gifts, the humans ended the conflict between Dragon and Witch. And there was peace once more."

Everyone has a place, Kaia thought as she sponged up the last of her stew with a piece of bread. She had been eating steadily and only now realized her plate was empty. *Balance is impossible without dragons, witches, and humans.*

"And that is how we all came to be," Mr. Luca finished. He smiled. "Once you are finished eating, you can explore the area, find a place to rest, or go swimming in the hot Silver Springs. You will each need to bathe before the ceremony tomorrow, though. And no, rinsing off doesn't count. You need to use soap."

Kaia laughed. She settled back in her chair, full and content. She'd be happy just sitting and talking for a while.

"Tomorrow," she said. "Tomorrow, we will all know our place."

The girl next to her smiled. "We will. And it will be beautiful."

CHAPTER
SIX

J udging by the amount of chatter throughout the night, Wickham wasn't the only one who couldn't sleep. He couldn't keep his eyes closed; he tossed and turned all night, trying to get comfortable.

Four new people greeted them in the morning. They were all older, with grey hair and wrinkled faces. These four introduced themselves as the headmasters of the four primary branches of the Academies. A thrill shot through Wickham as he looked at them eagerly. One of these people would be his teacher once this was over.

His stomach started cramping with nerves at this thought. Whatever school he went to would take him away from his family.

"Today is a significant day for you," headmaster Valiant said. "From here on, you will know your place in our Kingdom. We will call your name, and you will follow the headmaster to the Spring, where you will drink. Once we know if you are a dragon, witch, or human, you will be placed in a new camp to begin your training."

Headmaster Twila, standing next to Valiant, opened a scroll. "First on our list is... Wickham."

A jolt coursed through him as if he'd just been punched in the stomach. Was he first? Why? Trembling, he started forward. His eyes were so wide he thought they might pop right out of his skull.

The headmasters smiled kindly at him. Headmaster Everett, one of the human headmasters, gestured for him to follow.

"Are you excited?" the headmaster asked as they passed through the back doors of the stone building.

"No," Wickham replied honestly. "I want to get back home."

Everett laughed. "I remember when I drank from the Spring. I tried to pretend I was sick to avoid it; I was so afraid. But it is a wonderful feeling, Wickham."

Wickham wasn't entirely convinced. He pressed his hands together as they stepped into a circular room. A natural pool sat in the middle of it, bubbling slightly. A mirror stood on the other side of the pool. He took a deep breath and knelt beside the pool, then accepted the cup offered to him.

Closing his eyes, he filled the cup and then drank.

PENELOPE THOUGHT she might go crazy before her name was called. She tried her best to stay calm. She kept talking with the other children to ensure they were doing all right. Every time a headmaster returned alone, her heart jumped to her throat.

Please just let me get this over with!

"Penelope," headmaster Twila called.

Penelope jumped from where she was seated and raced to the headmasters. She had to dodge other children as she did so. When she skidded to a stop before them, she wasn't sure if her sudden burst of speed or her nerves had her heart pounding so hard. She stood up as straight as she could.

"I'm Penelope," she said.

Headmaster Twila smiled at her and handed the scroll to headmaster Valiant. "Come with me, then."

Penelope would have loved to run ahead, to get to the Spring and drink before Twila even got there. That would have been exceedingly rude, though, so she held herself at the same pace as the aged headmaster.

"You're Ellen and Mike's daughter, yes?" Twila asked. "Julie and Benton are your older siblings?"

"Yes. And I know you; I've been to their graduation ceremonies and would have recognized you even if you didn't have silver eyes," Penelope replied. She smiled up at the dragon headmaster. "I know I will be in your school as well. I must be a dragon."

Twila hummed. "What will you do if you are not?"

"I... I'm a dragon," Penelope said doubtfully.

"I was certain I was human before I drank. I had to adjust my entire life plan."

Penelope straightened her shoulders. "I won't. I'm a dragon."

They reached the Spring shortly. Penelope waited patiently as Twila retrieved the cup and gave it to the young girl.

Penelope knelt, filled the cup, and drank. Instantly, a pleasant feeling swept through her, like coming into a warm house after playing in the snow for hours. She tasted spice on her tongue, and as she straightened and stared into the mirror...

Silver eyes stared back.

Penelope grinned as euphoria drove her to her feet. She punched her fist into the air. "Yeah! See? I told you—I'm a dragon!"

HERJA HAD BECOME SO ENGROSSED in her book while waiting for her name to be called that it wasn't until the headmaster stepped in front of her that she realized her name had been called.

Heat rushed to her cheeks as she scrambled to her feet, brushing off her trousers. There were only a handful of children who hadn't gone through the transformation yet. The others looked at her with jealousy.

She felt like telling them it was their fault they were so bored, but she bit it back. After all, sometimes even she couldn't read. At the start, she kept looking up and disrupting herself. It was only after several hours had passed that she settled into reading.

She followed Twila into the back of the citadel and immediately went to the Spring.

Herja cupped her hands to scoop up the water, but a soft cry from Twila stopped her. Heat rose to her cheeks once more when the headmaster handed her a cup.

"You are eager, aren't you? I don't think you have heard a single word I've said."

Herja dipped the cup into the Silver Springs. "I just don't understand why we should waste time talking."

She drank, emptied the cup, and immediately turned to the mirror. At first, it didn't seem like anything was different. Then, as her shoulder slumped forward, the feeling of being wrapped up in a down quilt settled on her. As she watched, the color bled from her eyes, replaced by silver.

"Oh," she murmured, staring at herself.

"Congratulations. You're a dragon," Twila said.

Herja looked at herself this way and that. "I... see. I..." Her mouth was parched despite having drunk so much water. She looked up at Twila, feeling small and lost. "What do I do now?"

"Now, you will go to the dragon's camp," Twila said gently. "And you will learn."

"Learn. Right." Herja straightened her shoulders. "I'm good at learning."

⁂

AFTER HERJA WAS TAKEN BACK, Kaia found she couldn't just sit around and wait any longer. She gathered everyone who was left and started a rousing game of musical chairs, with the help of the headmasters, of course.

One by one, the others left. Nolen was the last one other than her, who was taken. And then she was all alone. It took a long time for the other thirty-five children to drink from Silver Springs.

Kaia paced around, wiping her hands against her skirt. She had packed one to wear while she was here. She had been wearing her trousers for the hikes and was glad to be in something so loose and free again.

Headmaster Valiant smiled at her. "Tell me, Kaia, how are your cousins doing? I remember seeing you last year at their graduation."

"They're well, headmaster," Kaia replied meekly. "They've all started their careers. I look forward to joining them in the Kingdom's service."

The door opened, and the human headmaster who had escorted Nolen slipped back in. Kaia's mouth went dry as Valiant smiled. "It's your turn."

Kaia nodded. Her mind raced as Valiant led her to the Silver

Springs, telling her of his emotions when he made this journey. Kaia responded appropriately, unaware of what her body was doing until she drank from the Spring.

A gentle, peaceful feeling wrapped around her, and her hair had turned silvery-white when she looked in the mirror. A witch, then. Kaia smiled in satisfaction. So that's where her purpose was, to help and support others.

Valiant led her to the witch's camp. Eagerly, Kaia looked around to see who else was there. Adina was, and so was Wickham. He stood away from the group, twisting his long hair in his hands.

Kaia bounded over to him. "Wick! You're a witch, too?"

Wickham looked up, startled. "Oh! Kaia. Hi."

"Hi," Kaia laughed in response. She hugged him. "Look at us! We're both witches. That means we'll be in school together. Isn't that wonderful?"

Wickham shrugged. "I guess. I just... wish..."

"Wish what?" Kaia tilted her head to the side.

"Never mind," he exclaimed. "It looks like our lessons are about to begin."

CHAPTER
SEVEN

I t was bizarre to look around and see all the glowing silver
eyes around her, almost as odd as knowing that she had those
same glowing eyes.

A dragon.

Herja never thought that the roles of dragons were particu-
larly... intelligent. They partook in vital works concerning everything; protecting the Kingdom from rivals and evacuating areas in
danger from natural disasters to carrying giant bags of water to
refill cisterns emptied by drought.

But it was all so heavily physical. You couldn't just read a book
and know how to fly; you had to practice. And the thing about practice was that Herja couldn't just... learn on her own. This wasn't
what she expected.

Headmaster Twila brushed her long braid over her shoulder and
smiled at the young dragons. "I'm very pleased to see your bright
faces. Some of you may be surprised at this turn of events, but we
remember that Silver Springs is where Earth, Sun, and Moon

converge. It knows your strengths and how you can best serve the Kingdom."

Herja let out a shaky breath. She wasn't entirely sure that was true. She would do more research and reading and find out if there was more to being a dragon than she knew.

Sometimes dragons are teachers, she thought, *or ambassadors. And we have a dragon king right now. So, I still have options.*

"Does anyone have questions?" Twila asked.

"I do," Herja said, shooting her hand up at once.

Twila nodded at her. "Herja."

"What happens now? I mean, for all of us. The witches and humans, too." Herja bit her tongue even as she finished. She'd read about what happened next and had even prepared herself by studying the basics of training on this mountain.

So why had she asked that question?

"Headmaster Valiant will teach the witches. The other headmasters will divide the other children according to their interests to explain their options, whether with additional education or training in trades." Twila smiled at her. "Was that it?"

Herja hesitated. Every eye was on her, making her want to shy back. She took a deep breath, bracing herself, and said, "No."

Twila nodded at her to continue.

"It's just that... I don't think I should be a dragon. I thought I was going to be a witch. I'd be much better if I were studying and developing new spells and stuff like that," she said, her shoulders rigid as she forced herself to remain standing straight-backed.

"I see," Twila tilted her head. "Well, this discussion will be good for you, then. We will first discuss the duties dragons are expected to perform. Let us sit."

Herja opened her mouth to keep talking, but a sharp elbow dug into her ribs. Frowning, she glanced over at Penelope.

"That's enough," Penelope whispered. "Twila knows what she's doing. She's done this for years."

"But she wants to talk about what all of you can do. I'm—"

"A dragon, just like the rest of us," Penelope interrupted. "It's not all about you, Herja. I get it; you're smart. Stop thinking about what that means for you and start thinking about how you can use your smarts to help other people."

Herja stared after her, hurt. That wasn't fair. Penelope didn't even know her. How could she talk like that, as though Herja was stealing and keeping everything for herself? She didn't think that everyone else didn't deserve their answers... she just had different needs.

But Penelope was right about one thing. With only one teacher, Herja couldn't get the attention she wanted. So, she pulled a notebook and charcoal pencil from her bag and sat at the back of the group.

Maybe if she took notes, she'd be able to answer some of these questions still plaguing her.

WICKHAM LEANED against the cool stone wall at the side of the group. Kaia sat next to him, almost vibrating with attention as headmaster Valiant spoke.

I wish I could have her enthusiasm, he thought as he wrapped his arms around himself. He hadn't expected to feel exhausted today when they had done no physical exertion.

But every time he caught sight of the silver of his hair, it hurt his chest. Why had the Spring made him a witch? He would have been happy to be human and would have been glad to stay as he was. Was he even still Wickham?

"A witch's primary responsibility is to help others," Valiant told the children. "We heal, we support, we nurture. Many of you will see these traits already when you think about them. If you can't see that inside yourself, don't worry. We are supportive, but that support can come in many forms."

"Wick?"

Wickham jumped, unaware that Kaia had been watching him. "Oh. Yes?"

She frowned as she looked at him. "Are you okay?"

"I... not really," he answered truthfully, speaking in a whisper. "I don't want to be a witch. I was hoping to be human. I wanted to stay home... my family needs me."

Kaia put an arm around his shoulder. "It's going to be okay. Your family will be all right. The Crown will take care of them."

Wickham shook his head slightly. He knew that there was Crown-funded childcare for his siblings, but Kaia didn't understand what it was to be the oldest. She was an only child. "The Crown can't tuck my baby sister into bed at night. They won't stop my brothers from fighting when Father has one of his headaches."

Kaia rubbed his back. "I'm sorry. It must be hard to think about leaving them."

It was—but it also helped him feel better, knowing that Kaia could see it was difficult. Sometimes he felt as though nobody else understood him. At least one other person could understand why he couldn't think about going to the Institute, even if all witches and dragons did the same.

"Now," Valiant continued, speaking a little louder as though he knew that not all his students were paying attention. "Can anyone tell me about a witch's duties?"

Kaia raised her hand.

"Kaia?"

"The most popular jobs for witches are herbalists, medics, and agriculture or horticultural assistants. But they can also be teachers, librarians, or diplomats," she replied, listing things off in a crisp, clear voice.

Valiant chuckled. "That's exactly right. Can anyone else tell me about our other jobs?"

Wickham glanced over the others. Nobody raised their hand.

"You can also be an artist, a writer, a farmer, a cook, a stay-at-home parent, a cleaner, a construction worker...." Valiant lifted his hands toward them. "Being a witch doesn't mean you have to go into certain jobs, just that your skills will be more suited toward those jobs. Once you have graduated from the Institute, you can pursue whatever path will be most fulfilling to serve the Kingdom."

Wickham straightened. The herbalist in his hometown was a witch... why hadn't he thought of that? The herbalist was often busy taking care of sick people and livestock. They could use another one in town.

He could get a job near his family and help them and the community. A smile blossomed over his face. This time, when he saw his freshly silvered hair, Wickham didn't feel sick to his stomach.

Instead, excitement filled him. An herbalist. That was perfect. He knew why the Spring had chosen him now... and how he could stay with his family after graduation.

CHAPTER
EIGHT

Twila walked among the children, answering questions quietly. Penelope watched her, envious of her grace and beauty. She hoped, one day, she would have the same self-assurance that the headmaster had.

Sighing, she turned back to her partners. They had been put into groups of three, and she ended up with Herja and Nolen. The other two stared at each other, and Penelope felt like she was trying to referee a silent fight.

"I knew I was going to be a dragon," she said if only to break the silence. "Everyone in my family are dragon, except for my mother. What about you, Nolen?"

Nolen rolled his shoulders and turned his gaze to her. "Human. Except now me and my twin sister. We're both dragons."

"Which one is your sister?" Penelope asked.

But Herja frowned at him. "If your family are human, how come you said you were part of the Silent Marsh watch?"

"Humans can be part of the Watch."

"It must be like the Fire Watch," Penelope said quickly. "We have humans in our camps, too. Normally dragons do most of the work, but we couldn't run without the witches and humans."

Nolen's face brightened. "You're part of the Fire Watch? We had a camp come in once to help deal with some fires in the swamp... They were terrifying; with all the swampy gasses, they could have exploded at a moment's notice. The Fire Watch always seemed so strong and brave."

Penelope straightened. Strong and brave. Yes, that was precisely what she wanted to be thought of as. "I'm going to be part of the Fire Watch when I graduate from the Institute, too. It's a family tradition."

"Oh, I guess I have to figure that out, too." Nolen's face grew serious. "But I suppose I have six years to decide. I don't want to be too hasty. I would like to work with the sea; perhaps be part of the Storm Watch."

"They're tough," Penelope said fervently. "I met one once, and even I couldn't believe how big he was. What about you, Herja? Do you have dragons or witches in your family?"

Herja frowned. "I don't know. I'm an orphan."

Penelope blinked. "But you have to know who your family was."

"Not really. When my parents died, the Crown couldn't find any relatives, so I was put in an orphanage," Herja shrugged. "It is what it is. But it doesn't matter what I don't know about my past. I wasn't sure what I'd do now that I'm a dragon, but now I do."

"What?" Penelope asked. "Military? Transportation?"

Herja gave her a baleful look. "Queen."

Penelope couldn't help herself and snorted. "It doesn't work that way!"

"It does!" Herja said. Her back straightened, and she glowered. "I know it's not as easy as saying I'll be the queen. But I'm going to do what I need to do to be Queen. I'm going to get the best marks in the Institute."

"It takes more than good grades," Nolen challenged.

Herja lifted her chin. "I know that. I'm going to work in every sector and know everything there is to know about agriculture, trade, protection, and social structures. I'll take that knowledge into being a diplomat, and then I'll prove myself the perfect person for the job and be voted in."

"But why do you even want to be Queen?" Penelope asked her.

"Because I'm smart, I'll know how to fix problems."

Nolen wrinkled his nose. "What problems?"

Herja got to her feet. "The ones that need to be fixed."

Penelope and Nolen watched her walk away, and Penelope shook her head. "She's weird."

"Yeah," Nolen agreed. He focused back on Penelope. "Tell me more about the Fire Watch."

Penelope was more than happy to do so.

KAIA RAISED HER HAND, stretching it so high that her side hurt. "Headmaster, I have a question."

Valiant gave her an indulgent smile. "You can ask it in a moment, Kaia. Right now, I need to finish what I was saying, all right?"

Kaia lowered her hand again, huffing. They had moved outside once the heat of the day had cooled off. The class was now sitting in a clearing surrounded by towering trees. The bark was rough and itchy to lean against, but Kaia's back hurt from sitting without support for so long. She leaned back against the tree.

"Listen closely," Valiant said, lowering his voice slightly.

The few children chatting with one another fell silent, facing him.

"Our magic is different from that of dragons. They are made of magic and can wield it as easily as you and I draw a breath. It's different for us witches." He paused, looking over them.

Kaia held her breath as his eyes met hers, sure he was looking for something in her. A sudden fear shot through her. What if he decided the Spring had made a mistake? Was there a way for them to take magic back?

"A witch must create their spells. Certain tasks can be shared, but for the most part, you will have to develop your own way of using magic. But that time is not yet. You must complete your training at the Institute and craft your Book of Spells before you attempt anything."

Wickham lifted his hand. "What if we don't go to the Institute?"

Valiant considered him. "Unfortunately, there is no alternative. Your magic needs time to mature, and you will need continuous supervision while you learn to exercise it. It's not safe for your families for you to use it at home."

Wickham lowered his head. Valiant sighed and walked over, kneeling before the boy. Kaia felt her heart clench. She hadn't thought about it before, but while at the Institute, she would be away from home, her parents, and her cousins.

I've never been alone before.

She shivered.

"I understand that it's hard, Wickham," Valiant said. "But please understand the importance. We are looking to expand the Institute to have schools spread throughout the Kingdom, so students don't have to go too far, but it simply isn't possible."

Wickham nodded, hiding his face in his skinny arms.

"You will have two months every winter and four every summer to return home," Valiant continued. "The semesters are only three months long."

Kaia couldn't stand to see how sad Wickham was. She pushed away from the tree and hurried over to him, putting her arm around his shoulders. "There, you see? You'll only have to deal with three months at a time. And your family might come to visit sometimes."

She glanced questioningly at Valiant.

"Occasionally," he agreed.

There had to be something she could do to help his dismal mood... more children than just Wickham looked lost and scared now.

An idea came to her. "Headmaster, can you show us some magic? Perhaps fireworks?"

Valiant smiled at her. "That's an excellent idea, Kaia. Thank you."

He stood back and rubbed his hands together. As he closed his eyes, sparks appeared at his fingertips. He spread his arms wide, light arcing from palm to palm.

The sparks turned into butterflies, and Wickham clapped his hands. "When will we be able to do that?" he exclaimed. "Tara is going to love it!"

Kaia smiled. She'd made him feel better. Good. Because they were going to have a challenging few years—but in the end, it would all pay off.

CHAPTER
NINE

T he following day, the children were gathered together to return down the mountain. Kaia was excited to see all her new friends and where they had ended up. They had little time to catch up before the adults sent them on their way.

No matter. Going down was easier than going up. Kaia wove her way through the group, catching up with the children who became dragons or humans.

When she found Penelope again, she had to admit that she had missed Penelope's blue eyes. They had been such a unique color. But she didn't say it out loud—she had seen how hard it was for Wickham to get used to his changed appearance and didn't want to make Penelope feel self-conscious.

"You're a dragon, just like you wanted," Kaia enthused, clapping her hands lightly. "I'm so happy for you!"

Penelope smiled at her. "Thanks. And are you happy to be a witch?"

Kaia fluffed her now-silver curls. "I think it suits me. Do I look pretty now?"

"I... I dunno," Penelope said with a shrug. "I thought you were already pretty. The color is nice."

"You did?" Kaia bit her lip. "You're not just saying that?"

Penelope gave her a puzzled look. "Yeah. You've got a beautiful smile and heart-shaped face that princesses in stories always have."

Kaia put her hands to her cheeks. "I always thought I was just chubby."

"Why would that make a difference to whether or not you're pretty?" Penelope asked. She looked so puzzled that Kaia had to duck her head.

Of course, Penelope didn't have any interactions with other Kingdoms, Kaia thought. Mama and Papa worked in the agricultural sector, but their connections to the palace had brought Kaia into contact with children from other Kingdoms.

Now that she thought about it, only one person had said she could be pretty if she weren't so chubby. Those words stuck fast, though.

She shook her head once, trying to dispel those thoughts. "Thank you, Pen. Can I call you Pen? I know sometimes people don't like to have nicknames."

Penelope laughed even as she rolled her eyes. "Pen is fine. We should probably take a break now, though. We're making good time so we can rest more often."

Kaia nodded. She would not admit it, but she had felt the urge to relieve herself for some time. She took off her pack and left it with Wickham before she slipped into the forest, looking for a good, private place.

She was headed back to everyone else when a slight crying noise caught her attention. It sounded like a baby or maybe a kitten.

Kaia hesitated. She had heard a story once about monsters who pretended to be babies lost in the woods to lure unsuspecting people to their deaths... But this was Mount Eldavon. No monsters could be here, could they?

The crying got louder and tugged on Kaia's heartstrings. She headed for the sound, pushing aside brambles and branches.

After a few minutes, she came upon a small creature. It was the size of a house cat, its back half covered in fuzzy, tawny fur, the front half grey and fluffy with some feathers growing here and there. Kaia gasped.

"A griffin?" Kaia crouched as the little creature turned its head to stare at her. "Hello, little guy. What are you doing here?"

She had seen griffins before. The largest she'd seen was only about twice as big as this one, but judging by how fuzzy and small it was, it was a baby. She crept closer, holding out her hand.

"You shouldn't be here; you should be in your nest," she said. "Don't worry. I'll help you."

She reached to grab the baby griffon when suddenly a shriek sounded above her. The next thing she knew, something hit the back of her head hard. It knocked her aside, driving the air from her lungs. Something else came at her with the sound of a stiff wind, and she could barely lift her arms over her face before an adult griffon attacked her.

Its sharp talons sank into her arm.

"Hey! Get out of here!" a voice suddenly shouted.

The griffons retreated, and hands grabbed Kaia. They pulled her to her feet and dragged her away. The pain made it difficult to see clearly, but a flash of red hair told her it was Penelope who had rescued her.

"What were you doing!?" Penelope asked her after they had been moving for some time. "When you didn't come back, I sent the group ahead while I looked for you. Why would you disturb a griffon's nest?"

Tears welled in Kaia's eyes. "The baby was on the ground. I just wanted to help it."

"Help...?" Penelope shook her head. "Never mind. Let's get those injuries taken care of so we can continue."

PENELOPE QUICKLY FOUND a little stream to wash Kaia's injuries. The griffons hadn't done too much damage to her. Mostly they scared her and ripped her clothes a little. There was only a little blood from the shallow wounds, but Penelope cleaned the scrapes thoroughly and bound them.

Kaia was quiet the entire time; her head was slightly bent.

Once she was done, Penelope handed Kaia a honey-oatmeal bar. "You need to keep up your strength."

"Thanks," Kaia murmured. "And thank you for looking out for me. I was trying to help, but I guess... the griffons didn't know. They must have thought I was attacking their baby. I didn't even know griffons would attack people. All the ones I have met were friendly."

"They usually are. Even the wild ones often want to be friends, especially if you offer them something to eat." Penelope stood and glanced at the sky. It was getting dark; she had spent more time caring for Kaia than she had realized.

"Why did they attack me, then?" Kaia wondered aloud.

Penelope shrugged. "It's the fledgling season for the babies. The parents are always slightly edgy when their babies learn how to fly and keep falling. Maybe they'd had difficulties with another baby, or maybe that one was just a little bit too hurt, and you startled them."

"Oh. I didn't know that baby griffons sometimes fell out of the nest. I always thought that they just flew one day." Kaia gathered her things and pulled her backpack on. "Although... I guess it makes little sense that way."

"No, it doesn't," Penelope replied. She tried to control her temper, but it was so silly that Kaia wouldn't know to leave the griffon alone! "Weren't you taught anything?"

Kaia stared at her in shock. She opened her mouth, then shut it again. Her shoulders hitched forward, and a lead-sort of feeling twisted in Penelope's stomach. She hadn't meant to upset Kaia.

"Sorry. I guess I just got worried, and I'm tired," Penelope muttered.

"It's okay," Kaia said.

Penelope shrugged. It didn't seem like the right reaction, but she wasn't sure what to do here.

"I'll do better in the future," Kaia said, straightening up again. "Thank you for teaching me, Penelope. You must have learned much about the forest since your family is part of the Fire Watch."

"Ummm... yeah," Penelope said, a little surprised. She would be reprimanded if she talked that way to anyone on the Watch. "I know about forests. How to reduce the fire risk, and when a forest needs the fire to regenerate. I'm determined to be on the Fire Watch after graduation."

Kaia cocked her head, her eyebrows drawn into a V. It was like she had already forgotten about their argument. "Why is that?"

Penelope took a deep breath as she led the other girl back to the path. "Well, it's like I've already had thirteen years of learning all this stuff."

"I don't think so."

Penelope narrowed her eyes.

Kaia grinned at her. "I don't think you were learning about it as a baby."

"Oh, you know what I mean," Penelope said, knocking into Kaia gently. But the teasing helped her feel better. "Recruits usually take years to understand all the signs fully, and I know most of what I need to know already."

"That's a good point," Kaia agreed.

"Yes. So. I'll be part of the Watch."

Kaia hummed. "What if your fated mate belongs somewhere else?"

Penelope stared at the cobblestone path beneath their feet.

"You have your perfect match out there somewhere," Kaia continued. "What if they belong on the sea or in agriculture?"

"There are ways we can have both," Penelope mumbled.

"I guess. But—"

"But I'm too young to worry about that now," Penelope replied.

Kaia nodded. "I guess that's true, too. I hope it works out for you, though."

DARKNESS EMERGED before they reached the first cabin. Penelope was looking forward to some hot food and a night of solid sleep. But it was oddly quiet as they approached the cabin. There were no sounds of chatter, no adults to greet them.

"They're probably looking for us," Kaia said as she opened the door.

They saw the other children behind a giant blue bubble as they entered. Penelope stared. What was going on?

"Kaia?" One of the girls— Penelope had forgotten her name— scrambled to her feet. "We thought you had been taken, too!"

"Taken?" Penelope repeated.

The other children gathered on the blue bubble's other side. The girl continued. "Just after you left, we were attacked by soldiers with a flag from Odentia. They took all the witches and dragons and sent the rest of us on our way."

A chill stole over Penelope's skin. Odentia? "But... why?"

"Where are the adults?" Kaia asked intensely.

"They've gone to get them back," the girl said.

Penelope and Kaia looked at each other. The question racing around Penelope's mind also clearly shone in Kaia's eyes... what should they do now?

CHAPTER

TEN

Herja bared her teeth as the Odentia man she had labeled The Jerk came closer. She and the other children had all been tied together by a long rope around their waists. It would be easy to escape if she had a knife or a sharp rock.

Unfortunately, she had neither.

"Children of Sun and Moon," The Jerk started, bowing slightly toward them. "I apologize for the necessity of this."

It was as though he thought that after kidnapping them at sword-point and tying them up, he could fix their perception of him with a little false reverence.

At least they weren't in cages... not yet. Herja felt something was waiting at the mountain's base to urge them out of the Kingdom before the adults could rescue them. Odentia had been trying to get magic for decades.

"I understand these events have upset and confused you," The Jerk continued, walking back and forth in front of them. He wore rich velvet robes of deep purple trimmed with gold.

"Why are you wearing such fancy clothes?" Herja asked, her tone mocking. "Don't you know you're camping in the dirt?"

The Jerk turned toward her. A flash of annoyance crossed his face before he forced a smile. "Ah, little dragon. What is your name?"

"Why would you care?"

The Jerk's smile faltered. "I don't enjoy tying you up like this—"

"Then untie us," Nolen said dryly.

Wickham was tied between the two and frowned at both of them. "Stop it," he hissed.

"Why?" Herja hissed back. "I'm not letting them pretend to be our friend."

"Because—" Wickham started, but The Jerk interrupted him.

"Your friend is quite right," he blurted, as though he was afraid of losing control of the situation. "You shouldn't fight against us. We offer you the chance for wealth and the freedom your parents would never dream of giving you."

Herja ground her teeth. What was it with adults assuming that you had parents in the first place?

"Odentia wishes to offer you refuge. You would have a position of authority, a place of respect, wealth, and status," The Jerk said, walking before them. "You see how finely I am dressed? You will have far better clothes than this. You will have anything you ask for—"

"Except to be untied," Nolen said.

Herja grinned. She liked Nolen.

The Jerk took a deep breath and turned toward Nolen. "You will have all of this without the responsibilities your Kingdom forces on you."

"Responsibilities?" Wickham straightened. For a moment, Herja thought he would tell them all to be quiet again, but to her surprise, anger flared in his eyes. "You mean taking care of each other. Using our gifts for the common good. Not hoarding wealth and food, but making sure no person dies because they have no food or shelter?"

"I..." The Jerk faltered.

Herja got to her feet, though it was difficult. "You can't do self-less things starting from a selfish position. We will never join you."

The Jerk sighed heavily. "I hoped you would be reasonable children. But since you are not... I will have to punish you. You will all go without food tonight. Think carefully about what you choose for tomorrow."

THEIR CAPTORS WERE SO loud that no sleep would come, even if Wickham had tried. His stomach crawled with hunger, making him feel like he was going to throw up even though there was nothing to vomit. One other had found some crackers in their pocket that they handed out to the group, but they hadn't gone very far.

Herja jerked on the rope that tied them together. She had been chewing at it for almost an hour now.

"Stop," Wickham complained.

"Maybe we can pretend to go along with them," Nolen said from his other side. "So that we can get some food."

He looked longingly at the table just outside the Odentian soldiers' tents.

Herja looked up; the corner of her mouth was turning red from rubbing against the rope. "Absolutely not. Didn't you see them adding those blue flowers to the stew? It's poisoned."

The smell of the stew hit Wickham again. His stomach growled, and his mouth watered, even though he tried not to think about how good it would taste. "If they wanted to poison us, they would kill us, wouldn't they?"

"Unless they mean to knock us out to make it easier to transport us," Herja argued.

"Where are the adults?" Nolen moaned. "They should be here."

A voice spoke behind Wickham, making him jump. "The soldiers laid a false trail down the other side of the mountain."

He turned to find Penelope and Kaia crouched just behind them. His eyes widened, and he stifled a cry. What were they doing here? The Odentian people wanted witches and dragons... they would tie up these two as soon as they realized they were here!"

Except their captors weren't paying that much attention. Even if they were, would they notice two extra children?

Herja tugged off her jacket and threw it over Penelope's head. "Cover your hair. Nobody else has a fire on top of their head as you do; they'll notice."

Penelope silently tied the jacket around her flaming hair as Kaia held up a pack. "We found this. It's yours, isn't it, Herja? Do you have a knife you can use to free yourself?"

"Forget the knife," Herja said, reaching into the pack. She pulled out the bag that she had her books in. "We can use this to escape... I think. We must distract the Odentian soldiers long enough to get into it.

"Into it?" Wickham repeated. "How are you going to—"

"Don't worry." Kaia took a deep breath. "You figure this out. I'll keep their attention off you."

Before Wickham could ask, before any of them could even guess what she would do, Kaia had stood. She strode toward the soldiers.

"Excuse me," she called, her voice loud and clear. "Just who is in charge here?"

THE GIRL HAD GUTS, Penelope had to admit.

She watched Kaia from the corner of her eye as the witch approached the villains. Her appearance had the desired effect since the soldiers focused on her in surprise. Penelope ducked low behind Herja and Wickham as their leader glanced over the other children.

"How did you get free?" he demanded.

"Um, I stuck my stomach out when I was tied and then sucked it in to get out," Kaia replied.

Penelope tuned out the discussion as she took Herja's bag. "How is this going to work? Even if it's spelled for books, people are much heavier."

Herja pulled her water flask out and dumped it over the bag. Instantly, the stitched vines grew. More flowers blossomed, looking like they had been sewn there forever. Penelope watched in amazement.

"How is that working?" Wickham asked in a low voice.

"Every stream on this mountain has to have a connection, however distant, with the Silver Springs," Herja explained. "That means it would activate the magic left in the bag and expand it. I've read about these things."

Penelope didn't care so much about how it worked so long as it worked.

"I don't think you understand," Kaia was saying, her voice getting louder. Her hands propped on her hips, and she tossed her short curls. "You have no idea who I am, do you? Of course not...

because you thought you could waltz into our Kingdom and steal our children, and nobody would be the wiser."

"Go back to the others, little witch," the leader growled.

Kaia folded her arms. "Aren't you interested in what I have to offer you?"

"You don't have anything—"

"I certainly do," Kaia said. "I have magic. I'm a witch. Don't you want at least one prize you bring back to your Kingdom to be willing instead of a prisoner?"

Nolen growled under his breath. "What is she doing?"

"Buying us time," Penelope said.

Herja chewed on the rope between her and Wickham. Penelope stared at her for a moment before shaking that off—there was no time to ask what she was doing. Instead, she gestured for the dragon tied on the other end of the rope to come forward.

"The bag should be big enough to hold you now," she whispered. "Get in quick."

The dragon eyed her warily but wormed her way through the small opening. Once the other girl was inside, Penelope checked the weight; the vines were still growing, and it felt like she was picking up a piece of cloth.

She looked into the bag, where the silver eyes of the other dragon were the only thing she could see. "Are you okay?'"

"Yeah," the girl replied.

"Next," Penelope said.

This next witch had broad shoulders, and it took some time to wriggle into the bag, but after him, the rest of them could slip in quickly. It appeared the mouth of the bag was getting bigger and bigger.

Herja yanked at the rope between her and Wickham. It snapped, and she smirked. "There. I'll be able to help you carry it now."

Penelope nodded.

Nolen slipped into the bag.

Wickham glanced at Kaia. Just as he was about to start into the bag, the Odentia leader looked over. He jumped, crying out.

"What do you think you're doing?"

CHAPTER

ELEVEN

The leader grabbed Kaia's arm. She reacted on instinct, remembering the lessons her parents insisted she learn. She stomped on his foot, then jabbed her elbow into this ribcage. He doubled over, surprised, and she freed herself.

Another Odentian warrior came at her, but Herja was suddenly between them. She let out a scream that sounded like something that would come out of a horrible nightmare beast. The warrior drew back.

Herja grabbed Kaia's arm and pulled her. They raced back to where Penelope and Wickham were dragging Herja's bag between them. Herja caught one corner, Kaia took the other, and the four lifted it.

The ache immediately set into Kaia's arms. Even if this bag had magic to make it lighter, carrying all those other children was difficult. She clenched her jaw as they started back through the forest.

But the Odentian warriors were already coming after them. They would not get away; they were too slow.

The leader laughed. "Thank you for making it so much easier to transport—"

A roar echoed in the night above them. Kaia lifted her head to see dark wings blot out the moon. A thrill went through her—it was a dragon!

Fireworks like the ones Valiant showed them lit up the forest. Silver-haired adults poured through the trees while dragons swooped in from the sky. Kaia couldn't help but let out a whoop, even as she stumbled to carry the heavy bag.

"Let's keep going!" Penelope shouted. "We need to get as far away as we can!"

Kaia gritted her teeth, hoisted the bag higher, and pushed herself. Memories of when she had reached her limit on the stairs at the palace filled her mind; how much easier it was to give up than keep going. But then she thought of the children in the bag, waiting. She pushed herself harder, determined that she wouldn't be the reason they lost their freedom.

Just as she thought her legs would give out, they reached the cobblestone path. Her shoes caught slightly, and they suddenly stumbled to a halt.

"Who's there?" Penelope shouted.

A lantern lifted on the path below them. "Penelope! It's Erin."

Kaia gasped noisily. Erin came into view, along with her a handful of the other children revealed as humans by the Silver Springs.

"Where are the others?" Erin asked.

"In here." Penelope lifted her corner of the bag. "We have to keep going. We have to reach safety."

Erin stepped in and grabbed Penelope's corner. "You're exhausted. Let us carry this; you focus on returning to the cabin."

The other human children gathered around them. Kaia's eyes flooded with grateful tears when not only was her corner taken, but another of the human children put his arm around her, urging her to lean on him for support.

Together, they made their way down the path. Kaia was nearly falling over by the time they reached the cabin. Once inside, Erin pushed through the blue dome, which protected everyone inside.

Penelope pressed her hands into the dome, but it wouldn't budge.

"It's because it was made to protect us," Erin explained. "Only people inside the protection can go back and forth."

Wickham knelt by the bag, holding it open while the other children crawled out. They looked disoriented; a few had some bruising on their faces. Kaia flinched. It must not have been fun to be jostled around in there.

"Get some food and water," Kaia told Erin.

Wickham added, "And medical supplies."

"And a knife," Herja said. "So we can all free ourselves at last."

THE OTHER CHILDREN'S worst injuries were rope burns and a few split lips. Wickham got warm water and witch hazel to tend to their injuries. He thought about home, about how the twins, with their daredevil ways, often had worse injuries than this that he'd clean to keep them from getting into trouble.

Penelope stood at the door to the cabin, holding a long walking stick like a sword as she watched the night. Once he had taken care of the injuries, Wickham went over to her.

"Let me keep watch," he said. "You go rest."

Penelope shook her head. "I have to be on guard. I must be ready if they come back for us."

"Except you're shaking," Wickham said, pointing to her trembling hands.

Penelope made an angry noise and tightened her grip on the walking stick.

"You need to rest."

"I—" Penelope started.

Herja interrupted, making Wickham jump out of his skin—he hadn't even realized Herja was there. "You won't be able to defend anyone if you're too tired to fight. Wick is right. We need to rest. The witches can keep watch and warn us if danger approaches."

"I... guess you're right," Penelope grumbled. She handed the stick to Wickham. "If you see anything out of place, sound the alarm."

Wickham resisted the urge to salute her. "I will."

The night was silent as he took up a spot inside the open doorway. He used the stick to lean on, fighting off his exhaustion. Above them, the moon streamed with its brilliant, silver light. Wickham watched the clouds, searching for any that might have that distinctive dragon shape.

What would they do if the adults didn't come back?

He'd never been in a situation where he would have to consider that. His parents worked in safe careers. He wasn't like Penelope, whose parents fought the fires. How could she do it? How did she live every day knowing that one day, with the wrong gust of wind or an unexpected falling tree, someone she loved would never come back?

He was shaking with emotion before he realized Kaia was standing next to him.

"I don't want to do this," he whispered, his voice raw. "I want a safe job. My family needs safe jobs. I want us all to be human because we don't have to worry."

Kaia laid a hand on his arm. "I'm sorry that you have that fear," she said slowly. "I've never thought about what it must be like for you. You don't have any dragons or witches you're close to, do you?"

Wickham shook his head.

"I can't pretend I don't know how scary it is. But I know that the Spring chose us for a reason, Wickham. You and me. We're witches. This is our destiny."

Wickham's eyes blurred with tears. He had a few things he'd like to say to destiny in that case.

A shadow passed over the moon. He stiffened, then shouted that the distinctive shape of wings was silhouetted.

"Dragon," he yelled. "There's a dragon!"

Adults emerged from the trees. Penelope was there in an instant, snatching the walking stick back. She held it out defensively until Kaia called out.

"Headmaster Valiant?"

Sparks lit the night and the worn face of the witch headmaster. He bowed his head, and in the light, Wickham could see that the rest of the adults with him had silver hair.

"It's all right, children," he called. "You're safe. The soldiers have been driven away."

Wickham breathed out the tension he hadn't even realized he'd been holding. Safe. They were safe... and he was going to see his family again.

TWELVE

T he parents were waiting when all thirty-six children safely returned to the palace. Everywhere Herja looked were joyful reunions. Penelope, Kaia, and Wickham had walked with her down the mountain guarded by the dragons and witches, but now they were all running off to bury their faces into the shoulders of mothers and fathers.

Something seemed to tug in her belly. All these happy people were reunited with people who cared so deeply about them. It made her want to cry more than the Odentian soldiers kidnapping her.

"Herja, there you are," a relieved voice said next to her.

She jumped and turned just in time for Mr. Bryce to hug her. He hugged her just as tightly as any parents hugged their children. And Herja, just this once, hugged him back. Her breathing became ragged as she fought back the prickling in her eyes.

Mr. Bryce pulled back and put his hands on her shoulders. "Sorry. I know you don't like being hugged."

"It's okay this time," Herja murmured, twisting her hands together.

"Are you all right?" He looked over her dirty, torn clothes. "Were you hurt?"

"Well... no," Herja said, her brow furrowed. "I mean, you remember how Suzanne and I used to get into those fistfights?"

Mr. Bryce looked confused. "Of course I do. We were all on edge for weeks."

Herja shrugged. "Suzanne hurt me worse than this trip did."

She expected her caregiver to laugh, but he looked even more somber. "I'm sorry. We should have stopped it."

"You couldn't know the Odentia were—"

"I mean Suzanne picking on you. She was bigger, and we thought it was one of those things that children have to solve themselves...." Mr. Bryce shook his head. "I didn't realize that she hurt you that much."

Herja wasn't sure how to respond to that. Suzanne had been a terrible bully, but only when there were no witnesses. And it wasn't like their scraps had gotten worse than a bloody nose. And that only happened when Herja answered Suzanne's cruel words with her own.

"I'm sorry," Mr. Bryce said again. "We never should have left you to care for yourself like that."

"I... I don't know why you're saying sorry," Herja said, confused.

Mr. Bryce looked at her sadly. "Because it's my responsibility to ensure you know you're loved and safe, Herja. And I didn't realize how badly I failed you."

"I don't like you talking like that," she said stiffly. Herja pulled away from him and held her arms at her sides.

His lips twitched into something like a smile, though he still seemed sad. "All right. I'll stop, just so long as you are okay."

"I need a bath, but I'm fine," Herja grumbled.

As she glanced around to avoid looking at Mr. Bryce, that feeling tugged into her belly again. Though there were more humans than witches and dragons combined, so many families had nearly been ripped apart.

That shouldn't happen. Children shouldn't lose their parents, and parents shouldn't lose their children. She let out a heavy sigh, and another weight settled on her shoulders.

When she told Penelope she would be Queen, she mainly had been trying to get the girl to leave her alone.

"There's one good thing to come from this attack," she said aloud.

Mr. Bryce looked horrified. "A good thing?"

"Yes. Because I saw what Eldavon could be if it weren't for our magic and our righteous kings and queens. I'm a dragon, which means it's my job to protect others." Herja straightened her shoulders. "And so, I will. Not just the people in Eldavon but other Kingdoms as well. I'll be Queen one day and make the entire world a better place."

"Herja... that's not your responsibility," Mr. Bryce said gently.

She smiled up at him. "Yes, it is. I am not usually the one who handles it yet, but I will be in six short years. But don't worry about me."

Her smile widened as she looked to where Penelope was animatedly describing what happened to her family, where Wickham and his mother were still hugging, and where Kaia was dragging her parents around and introducing them to the other children.

She looked back to Mr. Bryce, certainty in her. "I won't be alone."

AFTER GOOD FOOD, a good sleep, and a good cry, Penelope was ready to take her leave from the castle. This quest was far more exhausting than she had ever considered. She had thought that the griffon attack on Kaia was unsuitably tense...

Now, she wondered how the Odentian warriors reached Mount Eldavon in the Kingdom's heart. And what was their plan afterward? It didn't seem like this was over, even though her parents assured her it was.

The four rulers and headmasters, Twila and Valiant, met with Penelope and her parents before they took their leave.

King Lantos, his silver eyes alight with pride, nodded toward her. "From what we hear, you took on a strong leadership role with the other children. You could ensure that all your peers could escape the Odentian warriors unscathed."

"It wasn't me alone," Penelope replied, blushing. "I couldn't have done it without my new friends."

"Yes, we heard that, too. We will commend them as well." King Lantos put a hand on her shoulder. "I thought you would be especially eager to learn that those warriors were all taken into custody. We are well on our way to finding out how they got so deep into the Kingdom and how they evaded detection on the mountain itself."

Penelope let out a heavy, relieved breath. "Good. I was worried about that."

"I understand," King Lantos replied.

"Were any of the adults hurt? I didn't get to see them all." Penelope glanced at Twila and Valiant.

Twila was the one who answered this time. "We had some broken limbs, but nothing that can't be recovered from."

"Good."

Da cleared his throat. "Headmaster Twila, since Penelope showed such bravery and strength already, is there anything you suggest we focus on in the coming year?"

Penelope nodded eagerly. "Yes, that will be good to know. Maybe I can work on track so that next time I can find the villains before they attack, and nobody will get hurt."

"I think what you need to focus on," Twila said slowly, "is enjoying your last year before you're in the Institute. The studies will be rigorous, and you'll leave behind many of your childhood delights."

Penelope frowned. "But—"

"You'll be an adult soon enough, child," Twila continued, a gentle look on her face. "For now, let the Kingdom's protection stay with the adults. Be a child. I can't emphasize how important that is."

Penelope folded her arms. "But I don't understand."

"I don't think children ever do," Twila laughed. She shook her head as she ran a hand through her grey hair. "I suppose that's just something adults make up so their childhoods seem easier."

Penelope didn't understand but decided not to say anything else. Twila would only end up trying to convince her to be a child, whatever that meant.

Penelope had more important things on her mind. Tracking. Hunting. Learning to fight.

The Fire Watch isn't going to be a stroll in the park.

THIRTEEN

Wickham's head knocked into Mother's shoulder as the carriage stopped. He groaned, not wanting to have yet another break for the horses. He just wanted to keep going. The soothing rocking of the carriage helping him to sleep. After so many days on the road, though, what he wanted was—

"Wick!"

Blinding light flooded the carriage as the door flew open. In a burst of energy, both twins leaped into the carriage, talking at once. Wickham just sat there in a daze, unable to figure out what was happening for a good while.

Mother, laughing, finally got the twins to stop. "Go on, let us out. We have a lot to tell you all."

Wickham stumbled from the carriage, fighting yet another yawn. He felt he could lie in bed and sleep for a week; he was so exhausted. All he wanted was his room, bed, and his younger siblings' peaceful chaos.

However, as the carriage driver got their luggage, Wickham

noted concern on his mother's face. It was the same look she'd often had on their trip home. At first, he thought it was because she was worried that more Odentian villains would come after him.

Now, though, she was twisting her hands as she looked at the house, and a shiver ran down Wickham's back.

"Mother?" he asked, resisting the twins as they pulled on him. "What's wrong?"

Mother's smile returned. "Nothing, dearest. Go on with your brothers and tell them everything that happened."

"I want to wait until I can tell Father and Tara, too," Wickham protested.

At that, the twins went quiet. They looked shocked, and Wickham could only watch them with growing dread.

Mother sighed. "I had hoped... but never mind. Boys, you go on ahead inside. I need to talk with Wickham."

What happened? Wickham didn't dare ask aloud. If he did, his voice would shake, and the twins would notice. He could feel himself shaking as Mother took the luggage and set it on the porch before returning to him.

"Let's go sit near the pond," she whispered. Then, looking at his face, she sighed. "Tara is fine. She's gone to live with Grandmother and Grandfather for a few months, but she's fine. Your father thought it was best since she hadn't been exposed to... his illness before."

"Illness?" Wickham repeated quietly. His world was spinning away, and he didn't know how to catch it.

"You know how Father has been feeling so tired lately?" Mother asked.

Wickham nodded silently. He thought it was just because Father had been working so hard.

"He's sick. He has water in his lungs, a highly contagious condition that takes up to a year to run its course. You, the twins, and I have all had it before, and once you recover, you can't get sick with it again."

Wickham remembered that disease. It always felt as though he was drowning, and no matter how much he coughed, he couldn't get a breath of air. He had had to breathe in a magical mist for months, and his lungs hadn't recovered for over a year.

"But... but Father will get better, won't he?" Wickham asked. He felt tiny and helpless.

"Of course. It's an easy cure, but it takes a long while. But you know how Tara is about taking her medicines. That's why we sent her to her grandparents for the time being."

That made sense. But... it also meant that for the next year or more, Father wouldn't be working. Mother wasn't yet established in her new job. How were they going to make this work?

"I'll get a job with the herbalist," he decided aloud. "I'll work while you are home and take care of the twins when you're work-ing. And the money I bring in—"

He stopped as Mother shook her head. She squeezed his hand. "Wickham, you don't need to consider taking care of anyone. I've already talked with the herbalist, and we have a payment plan in place; as for our daily expenses, we are already approved for addi-tional help from the Crown."

Wickham slumped back. "But I want to help."

"You can ask the herbalist to be her apprentice if you want to bring in a little spending money for yourself," Mother said. "But we will be provided for, Wick." She kissed his forehead. "My sweet boy. I wish you didn't feel you had to carry everything."

"I don't." Wickham smiled at her, but he was hardly hearing her words anymore. He would go to the herbalist. He would apprentice with her and learn how to improve his father's medicines.

He would make sure that Father was well again and Tara was

back home before he had to go to the Institute. He had to. Otherwise, he wouldn't go.

WITH A CAP over her short black hair and an actual dress over her wiry frame, Herja wasn't sure if she felt like a grand lady or downright ridiculous. She certainly didn't quite feel like herself, even though this was the outfit she had worn.

Mr. Bryce and his wife, Mrs. Gwen, sat on the other side of the carriage. They had been mostly quiet on the trip, but now that they had reached their destination, Mr. Bryce spoke.

"Are you certain about this, Herja?"

She didn't trust her voice, so she only nodded. Before leaving the castle, she had made this choice. It had taken a few weeks of writing back and forth to get the position guaranteed. It wasn't common practice for students to live at the Institute over the summer, especially not before they were even enrolled.

Herja had spent many hours crafting the perfect letters to the two aged headmasters and all four Kingdom rulers to ensure this placement worked. If she were going to achieve her goals, she would need to double down on her studies.

And, she reminded herself, *I will have to build secure friendships once school starts so I can trust them.*

If she were to have both, she would need to get a head start studying. She imagined that socializing would be much more difficult; The Institute had excellent training fields for dragons, and she needed to improve her physical performance.

Mr. Bryce opened the carriage door, stepped out, and helped Mrs. Gwen. He held out his hand to Herja. She didn't need the help, but she accepted it because it would make him feel better. At least, that's what she told herself. She wouldn't admit, even silently, that she was trembling in the high-top boots she'd bought.

I look ridiculous. I should have worn my clothes instead of pretending to be someone else.

Headmasters Twila and Valiant waited to greet them. After the pleasantries were exchanged, Twila focused on Herja.

"I hope you know this is highly unusual, young lady," Twila told her soberly. "Valiant and I always stay over the summer with the students that don't wish to return anywhere else, but children as young as you rarely live at the Institute."

"I understand," Herja replied. "Thank you for recognizing my abilities and allowing me early entry."

Twila and Valiant glanced at each other. "We are allowing you early access, yes. You will be expected to work, though your room and board will be granted to you. You will have access to the library and may sit in on classes as well... but you aren't being enrolled, Herja. Like your peers, you will start in a year."

"I... understand," Herja said doubtfully.

Maybe if she could convince them to let her take the exams, she could skip the first year.

"We only agreed to this because we were afraid you'd try to train yourself and get hurt," Valiant added.

Herja nodded once, though she wasn't happy to hear that. Oh well. She would have to prove herself. That was fine. She already had a head start being able to study and sit in on classes.

"I won't let you down," she said to the headmasters. Then, turning to Mr. Bryce, she found herself choked up. She wasn't sure what to say... so in the end, she just mumbled, "I'll make you proud."

And then she picked up her bag and headed toward the Institute, not looking back.

CHAPTER
FOURTEEN

I t was a terrible summer for fires.

Since returning to the Fire Watch, Penelope had had little time with all her family together. One of them was always on the front lines to take care of the burning forests, battling back the flames that endangered crops and homes. Now that she had gone through her ordeal with the Odentian warriors, she understood better.

That didn't mean she stopped wishing that they could all be together all the time, though. She had so many things she wanted to talk about with each of her family members.

Since it would be yet another year before she could start her official training, she couldn't wait to go to the Institute with its spiraled towers and ancient stonework. The building had once been the seat of the Crown; now, it served as a training ground for its protectors.

"Don't you think you're overdoing it?" Benton asked her.

Sweat dripped from Penelope's nose as she finished the second-hundredth pushup. "No. I'm not. I need to be stronger before I go to the Institute."

"They do strength training there, Pen." Benton handed her a towel.

Penelope mopped the sweat from her face and sat on the floor. Her muscles ached, proving Benton right... she had overdone it. Her shoulder hunched inward as she fought to keep emotion from her face.

"Hey." Benton sat next to her. "Are you okay?"

"I..." Penelope rubbed her eyes hard as her voice shook.

Benton was quiet. He sat there, not looking at her, letting her get her emotions back under control. That was the thing that Penelope appreciated most about her brother. Sometimes she felt like other people were a bit too pushy, but he always let her go at her own pace.

"Da and Momma are proud of me for being a dragon," she said.

"Well... we're all happy about it, yes," Benton said slowly. "Why is that a problem? Did you want to be a witch or human?"

Penelope shook her head.

How was she supposed to word this? It would still be many years before she graduated from the Institute. Plenty of time to make an actual decision. She didn't have to say that she was breaking their hearts today. She could lead into it.

Benton scooted closer and put an arm around her. "Penny-Benny, you look like you're trying to tell me something. Are you happy that you're a dragon?"

"Yes." Penelope's voice was small.

"So, what's the problem?"

"I... I don't know how to say it."

Benton passed her a water skin. "Hydrate, think a little, and start at the beginning."

Penelope drank, grateful for the water and for the excuse to be quiet for a bit longer. Her throat was more parched than she'd thought. The cool water felt good as it soothed the roughness. When she couldn't drink anymore, she lowered the skin.

Where was the beginning, though?

"I always knew I was going to be a dragon. Da's a dragon, you're a dragon, and Julie's a dragon." Penelope leaned into her brother's side. "I know it doesn't always work like that, but there was never a doubt that I'd be a dragon...."

She let herself trail off, gathering her thoughts. Would what she had to say make any sense to Benton?

"I always knew I was going to be part of the Fire Watch," she continued, and her voice trembled again. "I want to be. It's what I know, and I can help so much because I already can look at a forest and know what needs to be done with it."

"What's the problem, then?" Benton laughed.

Tears spilled over her eyes. She couldn't do it, couldn't say it. "Oh, nothing. I'm just a little overwhelmed by everything... and wishing I could be part of the Fire Watch already."

The lie sat bitter on her tongue, but she couldn't correct it. Benton laughed again and kissed her hair. He reassured her that the time would quickly come that she'd be on the Fire Watch with the rest of them, but Penelope didn't hear his words.

Because she would not be on the Fire Watch at all.

And her journey to protect the Kingdom was going to change her. She knew it would... and was afraid she wouldn't recognize herself by the end.

IF NOT FOR the color of her hair surprising her every time she looked in the mirror, Kaia wouldn't have thought her life had changed.

It wasn't enjoyable. She had expected everything to be different after she drank from the Sacred Spring. Colors brighter, tastes sweeter, and birdsong louder. Instead, everything was the same.

She still had difficulty marching up and down the stairs. She still loved her dresses and hated trousers. Mama and Papa still had to travel for work; more often than not, she stayed home while they were out and about.

"Not that I'm complaining, mind you," she told Madame Adora one day while she was supposed to work on her languages. "It's odd how expectations sometimes don't live up to reality."

Madame Adora looked up from her embroidery. "I should think that everything would be different, Kaia. Your entire purpose in life has been enhanced. You know better what your destiny is now."

Kaia waved her hand at that. "I don't think that it's anything new. It's like hearing something that makes so much sense; you must have heard it somewhere. I'm a witch. I'm supposed to support and help others. Isn't that what I've always done?"

"I... suppose I hadn't thought of it that way." Madame Adora hummed as she held her embroidery out. "But you made friends, you said?"

"Yes. There's that. Friends change life... improve it," Kaia said.

She rested her chin in her hands as she looked out the palace's window to the lovely rolling hills and swaying golden grasses. She wouldn't see this sight every day for much longer. Autumn was approaching. But she'd be back next summer.

"Madame Adora?"

"Yes, dear?"

"Do you ever wish that you had a different purpose? Do you ever wish you weren't human?" Kaia didn't look at her tutor as she asked the question. It seemed unbearably rude, but she was insanely curious about the answer.

Madame Adora laughed softly. "Yes. I wanted to be a witch, and I cried for weeks afterward. But I love my life. I have had much happiness, as you will in your role."

"I'm worried that some of my friends won't be happy in their roles." Kaia straightened, an idea coming to her. "I need to write to Papa. He's got friends in the Census, right? Maybe they can help me get the addresses of my new friends. We can all write letters to each other."

"That sounds delightful," Madame Adora said.

Kaia grinned, carefully tearing a page from her notebook. She started scribbling her first letter. They could all write to each other, and when school started next year, it would be like meeting old friends rather than trying to get to know one another again.

It was perfect.

"I can't wait for school to start!"

The End

Read **The Quest for the Emerald Rattleback**, the first book in the **Defenders of the Realm series!**

If you enjoyed this book, please consider leaving a review on Goodreads, Bookbub or your favorite retailer. Reviews help me reach new readers.

Join my newsletter for writing updates, sneak peaks, review copies, sales, and giveaways at www.mhlebeault.com!